WHEN THE LIGHTS GO OUT

Edited By Byron Tobolik

First published in Great Britain in 2021 by:

Young Writers
Remus House
Coltsfoot Drive
Peterborough
PE2 9BF
Telephone: 01733 890066
Website: www.youngwriters.co.uk

Book Design by Ashley Janson

Softback ISBN 978-1-80015-627-2

Printed and bound in the UK by BookPrintingUK
Website: www.bookprintinguk.com
YB0485T

FOREWORD

Enter, Reader, if you dare...

For as long as there have been stories there have been ghost stories. Writers have been trying scare their readers for centuries using just the power of their imagination. For Young Writers' latest competition Spine-Chillers we asked pupils to come up with their own spooky tales, but with the tricky twist of using just 100 words!

They rose to the challenge magnificently and this resulting collection of haunting tales will certainly give you the creeps! From friendly ghosts and Halloween adventures to the gruesome and macabre, the young writers in this anthology showcase their creative writing talents.

Here at Young Writers our aim is to encourage creativity and to inspire a love of the written word, so it's great to get such an amazing response, with some absolutely fantastic stories.

I'd like to congratulate all the young authors in this collection - I hope this inspires them to continue with their creative writing. And who knows, maybe we'll be seeing their names alongside Stephen King on the best seller lists in the future...

CONTENTS

Frome College, Frome

Our Lady & St Bede Catholic Academy, Stockton-On-Tees

THE MINI SAGAS

MARIA

The church was warm and bright. Nobody expected their church to be haunted, right? "Lorenzo, por favor, Nonna will murder us if we set foot in there!" Maria shrieked.
"If," Maria's big brother replied.
Reluctantly, the girl put on a helmet and rapidly grabbed the flickering flashlight, before descending through the cave. As the shivering child tiptoed through the rocky, never-ending hole, two passages appeared. Thoughts flooded over poor Maria, wondering where her brother entered, but were snapped by her scream of: "Lorenzo!" A courageous Maria yelled, purely off adrenaline.
A figure appeared. "Addio," Lorenzo whispered, pulling out a knife...

Angelina Carieri (12)
Bristnall Hall Academy, Oldbury

MYSTERY LIES BENEATH US

Why are we here? I thought.
"Notaod, hurry up, we need to get out of this nightmare!" shrieked Michael. The second I heard that, the gravestones crumbled again. We got to a safe place... for now.
"Are we all here?" asked Adrien.
"Where's Jacob?" I cried. We looked outside. Blood covered the grass. I ran to the gate. Again, a scream.
"T-t-they are awake," I stammered.
As we tried to open the gate with our slippery hands, we heard it. "Never leave!" A deep voice covered the graveyard as the corpses dragged Jacob away.
"This was the worst idea ever!"

Charlotte Walden (12)
Bristnall Hall Academy, Oldbury

TRANSFORMATION

Disturbances were near. Me and Melody ran as fast as cheetahs through the empty, abandoned streets. I said, "Head to the park, I know someone there." We ran to the park but slipped on the hazardously slippery ice. Surprisingly, we found the hut.
"Mr Green," Melody said desperately. Our results were ineffective. *Crash!* The threat was choking us, just as Melody started to shake and ache fearfully. Melody started transforming into a human-like leopard. There was an explosion of light. "Melody?" I worried, fearfully. Melody was nowhere to be seen after the light explosion. I ran fast to find her...

Lewis Caswell (15)
Bristnall Hall Academy, Oldbury

THE DREAM

It's October 31st. Halloween. You're in an abandoned mental asylum. An eerie smell floats through the hallways and a shallow mist creeps through the windows. You hear footsteps but choose to ignore them. As you carry on exploring, you feel like you're being watched; eyes piercing through your soul and teeth daggering through your heart. The noises get faster and closer. You quickly run into a room. The handle starts to turn and a figure emerges. They drag you across the floor and you let out a blood-curdling scream. Suddenly, you hear an alarm go off.
It was another dream...

Lily Slimm (12)
Bristnall Hall Academy, Oldbury

THE MIRROR SAID

It was a normal school day. In the canteen, me and three mates were playing truth or dare. Dare, I chose. "Look in the mirror and say hello." *Pretty easy,* I thought to myself. How wrong I was. So, there I was in the bathroom ready to easily complete the dare. Little did I know, my grandad died from a heart attack 20 years ago whilst staring into the mirror. Anyway, there I was staring into the mirror. "Hello?" Then what happened next scared me for life.
"Hello?" said an old man behind me. The lights flickered.
"Help!" I screamed...

Austin Billingsley (12)
Bristnall Hall Academy, Oldbury

THE WARDROBE

The thunder raged. Cautiously, I opened the door. Someone breathed my name. As I ascended the staircase, hardly able to see, the voice grew louder. I slipped at the top of the staircase. As I stood, I noticed the thick, reddish substance on the floor. I looked up, staring at what I thought was a wardrobe. *Clink!* Someone was climbing the staircase. I looked back and forth. Stairs, wardrobe. *Thud!* The wardrobe rattled. The lightning sizzled outside. My hand trembling, I reached for the handle. I opened the door, blinded by a bright light. "Get up!" Mum shouted.

Aimee Houghton (12)
Bristnall Hall Academy, Oldbury

THE JEWEL

I walked into the house. Fog and mist were everywhere. "Arghh! Who's there? Come out! Show yourself!" The storm was getting worse. Lightning crashed down. Rain smacked against the window. Torrential rain. I walked up the stairs. *Creak! Creak!* I felt something or someone around me. I sensed this by the sudden cold air that went through me. I had ice in my veins, it didn't bother me. I carried on. Second floor. I made it. I scurried to find the jewel. I walked into a cold room. There was a box. Jackpot! I opened the box. "Arghhh! I'm trapped!"

Connor Craig (15)
Bristnall Hall Academy, Oldbury

THE GREAT MYSTERY OF THE OLD MANSION

They heard whispers from the house. "Help." As they approached the house, thunder struck them.
Later that night, they found themselves inside the mansion. It was dark and gloomy. The only source of light was the moon glimmering through the boarded window. Thunder was lashing outside. They all went looking for light sources. They found three torches. One of the torches went out. When it switched back on, he saw red liquid was leaking from under the door. The boy opened the door. All of a sudden, his friend was dragged into the cupboard and was never seen again...

Aaron Tyler Higgs (12)
Bristnall Hall Academy, Oldbury

THE DARK FIGURE

It was a dark and foggy night by the church. Jeff said, "No, Jamal, the church is off-limits and I'm not religious."
Rico said, "Oh, hell to the no! You can go, but I'm not!"
As they went in, they heard a crow. Then they heard branches snapping and bushes rattling. Jeff was scared. He shivered in fear when they saw a big, dark figure. As they ran further into the church, Jeff said, "Hold up, let's take our shoes off to show our respect." They ran and ran, then they jumped into a cold closet in fear. "Who was that?"

Ricco Wilson (12)
Bristnall Hall Academy, Oldbury

A DREAM OR A NIGHTMARE?

Knock! Knock! Knock! The breeze in the silent, dull room felt like ice. I could feel my heavy breath. The squeaky, creepy door opened. A person or a thing covered in black showed up with a black bag. "Who are you?" I said whilst quivering. Suddenly, it all went dark and gloomy. "Where am I?" I said silently.
"Silence! You have two minutes to figure out how to get out of here before you drown!"
"What? No!" I couldn't breathe. Then it went all dark again. "Help! Oh!" It was a dream. No, it was a nightmare.

Samira Aboubacar (11)
Bristnall Hall Academy, Oldbury

ABANDONED HOSPITAL

You are in a flower-filled field. Menacingly, you look to the right. A hospital stands there. You run over to the hospital. You enter. There are corpses lying in wheelchairs covered in bandages. You come closer and a bandage-covered creature whispers into your ear, "Run." The doors close. The creatures stand up and start taking off their bandages. They are all green. You are trapped in the corner. You recognise the creatures and you try to talk to them. They bite your limbs off, one by one. They start putting bandages on you. You scream for help. No one helps.

Oliver Wielogorski (12)
Bristnall Hall Academy, Oldbury

THE LOOP

As you walk past the abandoned house, you see a beautiful, blinding light coming from inside. You can't go in now, it's too sunny. Someone will notice and call the cops. You wait and go back eight hours later.
It's 11.59pm and everyone's asleep. You sneak out. As you arrive, you start to feel dizzy. As you step onto the lawn, you drop to the floor. Your vision's blurry but you can still see a faint figure. You've fallen asleep. You wake up and check the date. It's the same day as yesterday... Could it be? No. It's not possible.

Brooke Fulford (12)
Bristnall Hall Academy, Oldbury

THE TWISTED PARTY

Your parents keep waking up. Every year, same time, same day, same reason, but you just don't know why. Why could they be doing this? They go downstairs, light millions of candles and put them around the house. Could it be someone's birthday? But whose? Surely if it was someone's birthday, they would tell you. The colours of the decorations were your favourite. What could this possibly mean? You watch your parents as they invite a bunch of people that they met on Facebook. Little do you know, everyone's celebrating the anniversary of your death.

Olivia Lewandowska (12)
Bristnall Hall Academy, Oldbury

SHE CAME BACK

That odd night, he knew something would happen. The moon was gleaming on the church's graveyard. It was soaking in its light. He heard a sound. He ran into the church, frightened. The door slammed behind him. There was a shadow. He heard a blood-curdling voice. He knew it was her. She'd come for him! He ran through the endless path of darkness and saw the light calling for him. He heard hair-raising music but he kept going. He finally reached the graveyard and was relieved. Suddenly, he saw her. She was coming for revenge. She leapt and grabbed him...

Avneet Singh (12)
Bristnall Hall Academy, Oldbury

WHISPERS OF THE DEAD

Gasping, I darted towards what looked like an old house in the wet fog. Eventually, I stepped into the house. The door slammed behind me and I was locked in. The cackles and sounds of smashing glass began to grow louder. Gusts of wind entered the room with the cackling. Reluctantly, I walked towards the noise and a ghost popped up to my face. For some reason, it looked familiar. I muttered, "James Daniel?" The ghost dashed towards me. I was defenceless. Little did I know, that it was me in a past life. Strangely, I can't feel anything anymore...

Alfie Knott (12)
Bristnall Hall Academy, Oldbury

THE ROPE

I didn't dare to go through the forest but I had no other choice. As I walked faster, the branches cracked like something was following me. I tripped...
As I woke up, I realised that I was hanging upside down in a cottage. "Where am I?" I asked as someone walked through the door holding a dead body.
"Ah, my next victim," he said with a sinister smile on his face. I grabbed the rope, stressing relentlessly.
"You'll never get out," he said.
At that moment, everything went black like I was unconscious...

Aimee Smyth (11)
Bristnall Hall Academy, Oldbury

THE BABYSITTER'S NEVER-ENDING END

An old, creepy man with a doll in his right hand stood at the door. Carefully placing the doll in her hands, he said, "Take care of her, she's a lovely little girl," and walked away. Throwing the doll across the room, she ran to the abandoned basement. She found it sitting with the television playing. She heard a child singing. As it got louder, it felt like someone was approaching her. She felt hands on her shoulders. She looked back. It was a little girl. The babysitter ran away. More girls followed her while they sang. "Hel-"

Palak Kumar (12)
Bristnall Hall Academy, Oldbury

THE UNDEAD

He walked past the gate and as the moon rose, it appeared that it was unlocked. He walked inside and saw broken leaves left behind from autumn, bare trees and wilted flowers on the gravestones. Curls of thin mist wrapped and ran through the graveyard. Patches of grass lay between the rows of the gravestones. A chilly breeze brushed his arm as he stood in front of a macabre gravestone that towered over a new, fresh, empty coffin. A lump formed in his throat. His hands began to shake. The tombstone said his name. Something grabbed him by the shoulder...

Amielia McKenzie (12)
Bristnall Hall Academy, Oldbury

I LOST CONTROL!

Sat on the wooden swings, the wind stole my breath. Mist covered my view. I couldn't see. There it went again. The bell rang and cried, begging for help. I could no longer see what was before the church of dreams. The broken twigs beneath me cracked as my feet brushed across them. The grass was as dry as the roof of my mouth. Sunshine was a hidden memory. Birds cried for closure. Gravestone upon gravestone, the moss covering those who'd lost their lives. That's when I saw it; a finger coming from the ground, pulling me into the unknown...

Martina Pembrey (15)
Bristnall Hall Academy, Oldbury

THE HAUNTED MANSION ON ELM STREET

The door creaked open. Me and my friends stepped into the haunted house, shaking. There was a rusty staircase in front of us. Noises echoed through the misty room. Haydn decided that we should ascend the staircase, so we did. Slowly, we walked down the corridor and saw a dark figure in the distance. It started walking towards us. Scared, we all started to back away. The figure was moving even faster towards us now. Running back down the stairs, Morgan got her leg caught in a broken plank... Sadly, we had no choice but to leave her there.

Amy Wilson (12)
Bristnall Hall Academy, Oldbury

THE EDGE OF THE WORLD

Me and the rest of the scouts were just settling into our camp when we heard a vociferous noise. Being circumspect, we intrepidly went to have a look.
Following the discovery of the dino-zombie, we were vexed at what we saw. Then the dino-zombie started chasing us. After trying to reach the zenith of the mountain and succeeding, we were oblivious. After what had happened, we were gasping for air and for something to drink. All whilst the dino-zombie was destroying anything in its path trying to catch us. I know. Crazy, right?

Anthony James Cockerill (15)
Bristnall Hall Academy, Oldbury

THE TALE OF TWO BROTHERS

How did it come to this? wondered Bill with lifeless tears cascading down his hollow cheeks. He laid on his bed as silence crept into his room, but then, just as he was closing his eyes, he heard words that changed his life. "Why, Bill? How could you, big brother?" Then an ear-piercing scream filled the church.
Seconds later, he found the bleeding corpses of his family on the floor. He recalled the sin he had committed. It was years ago. He remembered the screams of his beloved brother as he was buried alive...

Wishwa Karawe (12)
Bristnall Hall Academy, Oldbury

THE ABANDONED BUILDING

A scream in the middle of the woods. I panicked. I was suspicious as to where the noise was coming from and what had happened. Then I saw footsteps. I followed them, not paying attention to my surroundings or where I was. The footsteps disappeared. I was lost until I saw an abandoned building. The door slowly creaked open and I stepped foot inside the door. The door quickly shut behind me. There was no way out. I was trapped. I began to see shadows appear with bloodstains and handprints all over the walls and floors. This was the end.

Rania Al Nasri (15)
Bristnall Hall Academy, Oldbury

LOCKED

I've been locked in my thoughts for the past year. Alone. Dishonest. I never realised I was on my own as there was always someone lurking around the corner of the asylum. Sometimes, my head told me dangerous things and I never knew why until I blacked out and never went back. It took me to a paranormal place. My thoughts. It had shown me where I went wrong and how I got there: isolation, neglect and abuse. Every time I felt that way, the creature would consume my thoughts, take me into its trap and cause me some problems.

Chloe Lawrence (12)
Bristnall Hall Academy, Oldbury

THE RUN-DOWN HOSPITAL

As Ash staggered up to the front porch of the abandoned hospital, his shaking hand reached the handle and opened the door. Walking in, he could smell the stagnant stench of dead bodies. It was repulsive. He slowly strutted up the stairs of the mouldy hospital being careful not to fall. Suddenly, he saw a cult of vengeful souls that never survived. Then he woke up.
It was now the next day and his parents were calling him crazy. They wanted him to see a psychiatrist. When he finally saw her, he realised she was a ghost...

Ellie Farrier (12)
Bristnall Hall Academy, Oldbury

THE MYSTERY

One day, me and my friend were playing basketball on my driveway. Then me and Toby saw this unknown figure. We thought quickly and decided to run across the road to the forest. It chased us into it. We then decided to hide behind a tree. Whilst me and Toby were hiding, I glared into the distance. There was a building. Me and Toby walked back over to my house. We decided to go back at night. We travelled deeper and deeper until the plain building appeared. We heard screams. It was a mental asylum with dead and alive patients.

Logan St Prix (12)
Bristnall Hall Academy, Oldbury

PUPA'S GHOST

I ran down the creaking stairs. I was being chased by Pupa's ghost. My friends' bodies were impaled onto the bloody walls of the church. Blood was dripping into my eyes, so I was unable to see the dark path that lay ahead of me. I suddenly saw a little girl dressed all in black, pointing at a door at the end of the alleyway. When I ran through it, the door suddenly closed behind me. A fog appeared in the room. I suddenly heard singing around the room. Images of blood, torture and cannibalism flowed into my head...

Kwadwo Osei Bonsu (15)
Bristnall Hall Academy, Oldbury

HAUNTED FOREST

Arghhh! Something just touched my leg and made me fall down the stairs. *Bang!* Hello, hello? Can anybody hear me? Who is it? Where am I? Thank God, I got out of my house. There's a haunted forest right in front of me. Let's go and see what's in there. Hopefully, a bush I can crouch in so I don't get touched again. But what if there are animals? I need to get out of here before I get kidnapped.
A couple of minutes pass and I ask a man in a white van for help. I get back home and go to sleep.

Sean Payne (12)
Bristnall Hall Academy, Oldbury

THE SHOP, THE SOUND, THE SILENCE

The walk home from school was short but dangerous. Small alleyways and all that. Walking, walking. I passed a shop that was deserted. A noise came from inside. I walked inside without really thinking. Step by step. A figure was there, holding something sharp. Darkness.
I came round and saw even more figures, but this time, they were a bit clearer. One was a girl and two were men, all around their mid-twenties. One came close. Then it hit me. I was rat bait. I struggled and squirmed. No use. I was gone without a trace.

Megan Fereday
Bristnall Hall Academy, Oldbury

THE ANKLE

Sally was going up the stairs but she fell and twisted her ankle which caused her foot to break. Suddenly, a school appeared, so she hopped to the entrance in the hope of finding medical supplies. She opened the door and went in. She was walking for ages down the never-ending corridor. Then she finally found the infirmary that had a door of high contrast and it lit up the dark school. She opened it in fear. She found bandages and put them on. Then she heard a footstep that broke the eternal silence. Then she saw it...

Karam Sidhu (12)
Bristnall Hall Academy, Oldbury

THE TRAP

We all stood still, shaking in fear, staring at the only thing in front of us. None of us moved. It was like it had us locked in a cage and we couldn't escape. I began to shiver, struggling to breathe. Then I fell against the floor, but I had escaped. I crawled away, holding back my tears. The mud was all over me. Suddenly, out of nowhere, something appeared. My way out. I crawled faster, finding it harder to breathe. I was close, I knew it. Then it grabbed me. I hadn't escaped. I was now in its trap...

Haydn Field (12)
Bristnall Hall Academy, Oldbury

THE CREEPY ABANDONED HOUSE

At night, the mist on the moist floor started to rise off of the snowy, leafy floor. It started to turn into a massive fog cloud that engulfed the haunted house. Then a sudden light turned on. It normally had no lights on. It was an abandoned house, why would it have lights on? I saw a character. Suddenly, the front door opened. The mysterious thing walked out of the house. I was curious, so I headed into the house. I noticed that it was smaller on the outside than the inside. Then the door shut behind me...

Oliver Yeomans (12)
Bristnall Hall Academy, Oldbury

DOLLS ALIVE

A pandemic has hit. Everyone is isolating. I join my lesson. The teacher isn't here, so everyone is speaking. As I join, they stop speaking. One by one, they turn their cameras on, revealing their identities. They're all dolls, creepy dolls staring at me. I shut my computer and sigh in relief. However, it is short-lived. A hand reaches out and grabs me. Limb by limb, I can feel its wooden touch pulling me through. I make it. I am on the other side. The dolls are skipping around, singing. Where am I?

Dillon Smyth (11)
Bristnall Hall Academy, Oldbury

THE VOICE WITHIN

Exploring the school was our favourite thing to do. We ventured out, not finding anything at all, but that all changed when we started heading to the school hall. Then I heard someone singing. I kept this to myself, trying not to scare my friend. Then he said the worst thing possible. "I hear someone singing." My hands started to shake.
I said to my friend, "Enough is enough, let's go home!" He had none of it and ventured into the hall. What followed would haunt me forever...

Tommii Billingsley (12)
Bristnall Hall Academy, Oldbury

CRIMSON LAKE

The moon hung over the forest as the fog slowly crept in. I ran in fear. I screamed for help, tears streaming down my face. I climbed into a worn boat. I stood on it and cried for help, oblivious to what was lurking below. My boat was rocking. Then my heart stopped a second as I fell into the depths of the crimson lake. Something or someone clutched my foot and started dragging me under. I was low on oxygen. I felt my heart beating in my ears. Then I started to panic. My life flashed before my eyes...

Morgan Madeley (12)
Bristnall Hall Academy, Oldbury

THE DEADLY FOREST

I came across a creepy forest. It gave me shivers that
trembled down my spine. Sticks were snapping all around
me. I was scared. I saw a figure approaching me. I was
terrified, scared for my life. I called my friend Jessica. She
told me she was on her way. She took a whole hour.
By the time she got there, the figure had already caught me.
I fell, hit my head and passed out. I didn't know what was
going on.
While I was out of it, I woke up in my bed. I'm never going
back there again.

Alicia Richards (12)
Bristnall Hall Academy, Oldbury

THE GRIM TOUCH

Through the fog of the sequestered woods, I saw a clandestine figure for a brusque moment. Lurid. Surrounded by fog, I had nowhere to run. Whilst looking for the figure, it was then that I felt a cold touch and a swift breeze on my back. Morose. I tried to repudiate my doom but that wasn't enough. A shadowy figure towered over me. It wore a dark robe, but with the glimpse of my eye, I saw a hollow skull within. A hand reached out as my impending demise awaited me...

Aleksandr Fomkin (15)
Bristnall Hall Academy, Oldbury

THE NOISE

One night, I went for a ride on my bike with some friends. We went to the park and played tag. When we'd finished, we heard a noise: the scream of a child. We went to look and it was a doll. It looked creepy, so we went back. Then we saw the doll again, so we threw it in the bin. Then we decided to go back to my house. We were talking about the doll. Then the light flickered and came back on. The doll was right there, saying, "I can see you."

Danae Rouse-Clarke (12)
Bristnall Hall Academy, Oldbury

GRANDMA'S SPIRITUAL NECKLACE

After my grandma passed, I had her necklace. Even though I wear it every day, at night, it takes me... Whenever I fall into my slumber, I am transported into the infinite void of a deadly black ocean. There, I see my grandma smiling at me in the water. I always try to reach her to hug her once again. When I finally reached her, I never woke up again. I'm still waiting for my sister to reach me...

Skyrah McIntosh (12)
Bristnall Hall Academy, Oldbury

THE THRILL OF THE CHASE

I could smell something rancid, rotten, like death. There was something else though, a sweet smell too: holly berries. Leaves rustled as I sprinted through the forest, trees looming overhead, threatening to trap me. I had to keep running. Just outside my vision, I saw it. I could taste a bitter, acrid taste: defeat, but something else too, something sweeter: freedom. I couldn't stop; it was right there. Something howled; deep and gut-wrenchingly raw. Pure terror. I craved it. I desired it. I wanted it.
Finally, I had him. I'd caught him. Time for my freedom, my thrill, my fun...

James Comins (14)
Cansfield High School, Ashton-In-Makerfield

THE FOREST

My house had always been next to the forest. My parents always seemed to hate it but I was intrigued. There were stories about people going missing but I never understood why until one night, wandering from home, the moon guided my path amongst the trees as I entered the forest. The wind was like hot breath against my skin. The air was thick and damp. Then I realised that fog was slowly rolling in and my eyesight was getting worse. Suddenly, footsteps and whispers were all around me, cornering me. I heard a voice.
"Goodnight."
The hospital? What accident?

James Moreland (12)
Cansfield High School, Ashton-In-Makerfield

CURBSIDE PICKUP

The man walked alone down the empty country road. His bus had stopped earlier than expected. Out of the corner of his eye, he spotted an old 1960s style car driving towards him. He stuck out his thumb; the universal sign of a hitch-hiker. The car stopped. He stepped into the car and said, "Devon, please." No response. As the car drove on, the passenger noticed something odd about the driver. He wasn't there. Before he could scream out in terror, the car skidded around a sharp bend, crashing into the ornate graves in the churchyard where the driver lived.

Ben Sudworth (12)
Cansfield High School, Ashton-In-Makerfield

THE TOY ROOM!

It was late at night and Tom was playing with his Jack-in-the-box. "Tom, it is time to go to bed."
The boy replied, "Okay." Before he left the room, he heard someone whisper his name. "Come, Tom, come." Tom followed the whisper. Then he heard the whisper again. "Come, Tom, come." It was his Jack-in-the-box.
"H-h-hello," he spluttered.
The thing that happened next was very strange. The Jack-in-the-box wanted a handshake. Tom put his hand out and before he knew it, he was gone. Gone forever.

Ellis Whitfield (12)
Cansfield High School, Ashton-In-Makerfield

THE CREAKING HOUSE

I told them not to go in. There we stood, outside the dark, spine-chilling building. You could feel the mind-numbing suspense waiting for you to walk in. When you did, the death and blood hit you like a heatwave.
While we were creeping up the stairs, there was a crash of lightning like a gunshot. There she was. A tall, dark, slender woman walking slowly, followed by three toddlers screaming and yelling, but the woman kept walking peacefully. As we all looked shakily to our left, we saw a picture of a woman with her family. They were all dead...

Jessica Leyland (13)
Cansfield High School, Ashton-In-Makerfield

THE NEVER-ENDING NIGHTMARE

He woke up. It was the middle of the night. He heard a devilish scream and was curious, so went to head downstairs. He noticed that everywhere was darker than normal. "Mum?" No reply. He could hear a slight giggle. "Mum?" No reply. He was now downstairs and a figure was at the end of the hallway. It wore the same clothes that his mum wore. "Mum?" No reply. The figure stared, then disappeared. He woke up. It was the middle of the night. He heard a devilish scream. He headed downstairs. His mum was nowhere to be seen...

Jake Pimblett (12)
Cansfield High School, Ashton-In-Makerfield

DON'T TOUCH THE NECKLACE

It was all fun and games when I came across the old, beautiful necklace. It was from the Victorian era. I put it on. Nothing happened for days until paranormal activity struck. I heard a whisper. "Come closer." As I walked closer, I felt a stroke of air across my arm, then the sound of knives clashing. That's when the torture began. I woke up and saw a woman walking away with the necklace. There was no sign of the necklace again and the scars from the torture never left until she died and the necklace came back to my neck.

Emily Pollitt (12)
Cansfield High School, Ashton-In-Makerfield

THE SILENCE IS LOUD

The laughter of children and the chatter of adults surrounded the forest. The leaves crunched as the children ran after the football. The wind had started to pick up and a huge gust of it blew the ball into a large bush.
"I'll get it!" shouted a little girl. She crouched to try and see the ball, but it was too far in. She crawled in. Soon, the ball came out, but she didn't. In fact, she never did. The ball rolled out in silence. No one was there, not a single soul. At least, not an alive one.

Aaliyah Evans (13)
Cansfield High School, Ashton-In-Makerfield

THE CAGE

She woke up, scared and alone. Her eyes jolted open as if she had just had a bad dream. She looked around her as she let her eyes adjust to the darkness that surrounded her. Suddenly, she brought her attention to the metal bars that were around her. Confused, she reached out to grab them and was surprised when she could feel the cold metal against her skin. It was as if she expected her hand to go straight through. She was trapped. She panicked and shook the bars for someone to let her out. Then she saw it...

Faith Scales (12)
Cansfield High School, Ashton-In-Makerfield

DEVIL TOWN

Me and three of my friends slumped into the grey water looking for Grayson. *Splash!* Finn had fallen into the wretched water. Overlapped yelling broke out as Finn screamed and complained. I yanked Finn out. He was yelling and blaming us for dragging him down there. He smelt revolting with his shirt slightly tinted grey.

"Guys," Kali mumbled under her voice.

"My mum's gonna kill me," Finn interrupted.

"Guys!" Kali yelled. She pointed at a head resurfacing from the water, blood and gore spilling out. The familiar blonde's head spun.

"It's Gray! Th-that's-"

"Fake!" Max reassured.

"Am I?" replied Grayson...

Emma Campbell (12)

Fraserburgh Academy, Fraserburgh

THE FOREST

"C'mon, it'll be fun!" Chris cried out. "We'll go into the woods and play hide-and-seek. The last one found, wins!" Little did the group of friends know that a peculiar guest would be joining them in this fun game.
As the group of friends descended into the forest, the thick, white fog followed them.
"The air feels different here. It's as if the fog is eating away at my flesh." Their hearts paced as the wind picked up. Trees rustling, branches falling, wolves howling. Chris started to rethink his decision of taking them into the forest. Then the thing appeared...

Joshua Ileladewa (13)
Fraserburgh Academy, Fraserburgh

THE CHASE

It's been five years and I'm still chasing him through the galaxy and I've finally tracked him to the tomb world of the Necrons. I am Esinhorn and I've been hunting a plague marine called Typhon.
Running through the tomb world with thousands of Necrons in stasis along the long, dark and eery tunnels, suddenly a beam of light shoots past my head. I jump behind a Necron's body.
"Hello Esinhorn," Typhon sneers. "Are you here to play, Esinhorn? Hahaha."
"No Typhon," I reply as I fire an automatic bolt gun.
Suddenly a sound echoes down the corridor...

Alex Packer (12)
Fraserburgh Academy, Fraserburgh

CREEPY HAUNTED HOUSE

It was a black, windy, rainy night. He walked up to the creepy haunted house. He opened the broken, rotten door. He shouted, "Hello?" No answer. He looked around the hallway. It was cold inside. He called Jim. "I'm here." Jim answered, "I'm coming right now."
He sat down on the cold, rotten, wooden stairs and he felt a creak. He jumped off the stairs and looked around. Then he felt a touch. He heard a voice and turned around and screamed, "Arghhh!" He ran and tried to call Jim. He ran back to the car. It didn't start. "Noooo!"

Craig Marshall (12)
Fraserburgh Academy, Fraserburgh

HER NOT-SO-HAPPY EVER AFTER

She was still running. It'd been days since she'd had a good sleep. Maria never thought an ordinary necklace could cause the whole royal family to want her dead. As she was running, she could hear the leaves crinkling. This meant the royal guards were very near. "Halt!" she heard. *This is it*, Maria thought. She slowly turned around. Maria saw the bloodthirsty look in their eyes. She thought about her life. She loved her life as the Prince's wife. She never thought one mistake would lead to this.
When she snapped back to reality, there he was... her husband.

Keira Weir (15)
Fraserburgh Academy, Fraserburgh

THE ABANDONED MANOR

"Be careful!" shouted Bethany.
"I will," replied Robyn.
Robyn quietly opened the big, wooden door and entered the abandoned manor. As soon as she entered the manor, she noticed there were rats crawling everywhere. She started going up the grimy stairs. Nearly at the top of the stairs, she heard footsteps, so she started freaking out.
When she got to the top of the stairs, she heard someone say, "Get out, now!" She started running like a track star to get out of the manor, but as she opened the door, someone grabbed her foot and pulled her down...

Levi Blackhall (13)
Fraserburgh Academy, Fraserburgh

FACELESS

Slam! Emma heard her front door close. She slowly climbed out of bed. *Creak!* She froze. Something was in her old, stupid house in the old forest. She slowly opened her bedroom door. There was a tall, skinny, deranged, faceless figure. It kept twitching. The creature made a sudden fast movement and grabbed Emma. Her heart started racing. She was shaking and sweating. The creature started running with Emma in its arms. A high-pitched, creepy melody started playing and angry, muffled whispers started getting louder. It was too much. She wanted to just die... *Silence.*

Billy Jones (13)
Fraserburgh Academy, Fraserburgh

POV OF THE DEMON DOLL

200 years I've been waiting for someone to walk into this creepy, stinky, abandoned house. *Bang! Bang! Bang!* Oooh, someone has arrived. Time to scare them, so I can jump into their body and control them.
"Hello," said the man.
I responded by saying, "Hello."
Then they started running up the stairs, so I threw the mini table at them from the top of the stairs. They quickly moved out of the way but one slowly dropped to the floor and rolled down the stairs. So I quickly rolled myself to jump into her soul and control her. Then I jumped...

Kieren Ward (13)
Fraserburgh Academy, Fraserburgh

THE CRY FOR HELP!

"Joe... Joe, help me!" I could hear the faint cry for help. *I can't go down there,* I thought. The faint cry continued. Suddenly, I found myself slowly entering the doorway. Steadily, I descended the stairs. My heart was thudding against my chest. All of a sudden, my hand brushed against something soft and comforting. But at the same moment, a shiver trickled down my spine. I'd reached the bottom. My eyes were straining to see in the never-ending darkness. A shadow emerged at the end of the corridor. I was transfixed to the spot. What or who was there?

Emily Reid (13)
Fraserburgh Academy, Fraserburgh

THE ORPHANAGE

Walking through the halls of your new home, you feel uneasy. Something isn't right about this orphanage. You haven't seen anyone since dinner and now it is eleven at night. There are many rooms but no light, except the kitchen. Being the curious child you are, you decide to walk over. Your steps are gentle, trying not to bring attention. The sight of what's inside makes you feel nauseous. Children's bodies lie around on the old, white, tiled floors, decapitated and bloody. You slowly back up and walk back to your room. Now the calendar in the kitchen makes sense...

Elli Gorgon (13)
Fraserburgh Academy, Fraserburgh

THE STRANGER

"We'll have to stay the night," they said as they stood in front of this old, scruffy shelter. They unpacked their bags and settled in.
"That was a long journey," Caitlyn said in a tired and slightly scared voice. Suddenly, both of them heard rustling and rattling in the bushes not so far from them. Caitlyn and Rayan dropped in fear. They slowly started to sneak towards the noise to find out what the strange thing was. Rayan stood in front of Caitlyn to protect her and pulled out a pocketknife. Then something jumped out and started to attack Rayan...

Julia Noszczyk (14)
Fraserburgh Academy, Fraserburgh

THE DEVIOUS CREATURE

"Arghhh!" He let out a blood-curdling scream. Elizabeth ran to him, only to see him lying there lifeless on the floor. She ran as she knew whatever killed him would come for her next. As she turned the corner, she saw a message scrawled on the wall. She read the message hastily. It stated: *'He will catch you! Run, run, he's coming! He will get you, don't stop running!'* Before she could run, she was pinned down by the creature. The creature sucked the life out of her.
This is the story of the two hikers whose bodies still remain unfound...

Mackenzie Bannerman (14)
Fraserburgh Academy, Fraserburgh

IT'S COMING

Shadows dance in-between the graves. A figure emerges. Bursts of fog come running at me. I knew I shouldn't have taken the shortcut. I bump into something. I scream. It grabs me. I have goosebumps. I feel so many emotions rushing through me; regret, worry, fear. It's ruining. Daggers from its eyes hit me. Suddenly, it lets go. Without hesitation, I start to run. I see a building. My shaking hand opens the crooked door. I think I'm safe. Walking up the staircase feeling watched, the floorboards creak from below. It must be back. Windows shatter. It's coming...

Paris Ward (15)
Fraserburgh Academy, Fraserburgh

INTO THE UNKNOWN

It was Halloween. My friends and I went to the haunted house. We were all dressed in our scary costumes. We walked around the house. Then ghosts came running out in front of our faces. We were terrified. There was darkness everywhere. The lights were flickering. A clown came out of the corner. "Boo!" We all rushed up the stairs. Slowly, we walked around upstairs searching for the door to get out of this terrifying house. There was a door with a sign. It read: *'Do not enter!'* Lucy desperately wanted to enter. We all followed her into the unknown...

Sophie Muirhead (13)
Fraserburgh Academy, Fraserburgh

THE BLACK KINGDOM

"I'd do anything for my kingdom," said the princess while holding my knife covered in dark red blood and parts of skin. "Eww!" I shook my head as a black circle landed around me. *It's perfect, but what is it? Crows? Why crows?* I thought. Little did I know, this was the start of the black kingdom. I climbed the creaking stairs into my cold, lumpy bed. I looked under my bed - decapitated bodies? *That's it, I'm done.* I ran from my kingdom with terror in my eyes. I watched with a tear as I burnt my kingdom to ash...

Melanie Bolt (12)
Fraserburgh Academy, Fraserburgh

THE DARE!

At first, the rumours didn't convince you and you thought it was just a dare. Until one dark, misty night, you opened the heavy, creaky door in search of a book you were instructed to retrieve. Rumours said that the thin pages of the ancient book held evil and dangerous spells.
Suddenly, lightning struck, illuminating the cold room, showing ghostly figures. You anxiously ran up the steep stairs with the feeling you were being watched. Finally, you found what you were searching for, but the second you picked it up, you disappeared. The book was left on the table...

Andie Watt (12)
Fraserburgh Academy, Fraserburgh

FOOTSTEPS

I darted around the corner, feet crunching in the snow. I ran for what felt like hours through the dark, abandoned garden of the unusual house. Finally, I found a door. Locked. I tried to pick the lock but the footsteps were getting louder and closer, closer, closer... *Click!* The door swung open. I ran as fast as I could, stairs creaking. There had to be someone there who could help me. Then I heard the stairs creaking. I started panicking, yelling for anyone to help me. I hid under the bed, feeling safe. Then something covered my mouth.
"Hello..."

Ellie McKinstry (12)
Fraserburgh Academy, Fraserburgh

STAYING THE NIGHT

"We'll have to stay the night," said Susan as she turned to face Tom.
"We can't, look at the roof!" Susan looked up and saw that the stained wallpaper was hanging, weighed down by water. They knew that they couldn't stay there for long, but they had no choice. They couldn't go anywhere else because they were in the middle of nowhere. They started to unpack and got ready to go to sleep.
Halfway through the night, *drip, drip, drip!* Susan woke up and looked at the roof. She saw a hole. Not just any hole, it was...

Sarah Melvin (14)
Fraserburgh Academy, Fraserburgh

THE HOUSE OF PAINTINGS

"Sandy, you know you shouldn't go into the house, it's dangerous." But before he had time to stop him, he'd gone. Tentatively, Sandy crept down the steep stairs to be stopped by a dead body at the door. He examined it closely and then walked by it. He then pushed open the old, rotten door. After that, he explored the derelict house. There were large, ripped paintings all over the walls. Sandy quickly ran up the wooden stairs as he thought he was being watched by the creepy paintings. When he reached the top, he heard the wooden door slam...

Aiden Buchan (12)
Fraserburgh Academy, Fraserburgh

THE STAIRCASE

She was pale and trembling like a leaf. I'd met a small, old woman stumbling towards me as slow as a snail. We entered the building and saw a cracked, stone staircase and blood dripping from the roof. The woman didn't look frightened and seemed like she knew where she was going. She seemed to be leading me onto the spooky, stone staircase that smelt of decay. Frightened, I started to hear screaming coming from under the staircase. I took a step onto the staircase, shivering. I heard a bang and a quiet whisper. "You fell right into our trap..."

Aiden Robertson (14)
Fraserburgh Academy, Fraserburgh

HUNTING YOURSELF DOWN

He sprinted, chasing the brown-haired girl down the dark, gloomy street, unaware of his own capabilities. A detective during the day, a murderer at night. Hunting himself down, trying to solve his own murders. He knew the girl, Gorgeous, he knew her very well. In fact, she was his best friend. He picked up his pace and grabbed her arm with a firm grip. He reached into his back pocket, reaching for the blade. He pinned her down and sank the knife into her. Blood gushed out. He then said very softly, "Wasn't red your favourite colour, dear Emily?"

Kaelyn Simpson (13)

Fraserburgh Academy, Fraserburgh

RUNAWAY

The hallway was dirty, crooked and bloodied, but I couldn't let the demon lay his filthy claws on me. I kept running down the ominous corridor, feeling the cold, stinky breath of the monster tingle down my spine. *Crack!* The rotten planks of wood kept shattering at my feet, but I didn't stop. I dashed past a rusty, metal door. I continued running down what seemed like an endless, tight route until the fog unveiled a smashed window I'd fall out of if I kept running. I had to act fast. I slid beneath the creature and started going back...

Marcel Spyrka (13)
Fraserburgh Academy, Fraserburgh

THE CHASE

There I was, running through the dark, damp forest. The sound of thunder filled the air. Flashes of lightning struck. I tumbled to the ground, blood pouring from the gash in my leg. I quickly got back up and hid behind a tree, frantically trying to stop the bleeding. He was there now. The snapping branches got louder and closer. Trying to be silent, I held my breath to disguise the panting. I could hear him. "Come on darling, I know you're here!" Silence. Was I safe now? Unexpectedly, a cold, rough hand reached out and grabbed my neck...

Hannah Gerrie (15)
Fraserburgh Academy, Fraserburgh

THE HALLWAY

I slowly reached out and turned the loose handle. The hallway was dusty and there were bloody handprints down the walls. I looked up. There were huge, smashed skylight windows. The carpet was white with a massive dirt stain. On the shelves, there were rats; some alive and some dead. As I stepped onto the first step, it creaked. I quietly and slowly walked upstairs. My hands and legs were shaking. Upstairs was very eerie. All over the roof and walls, there were big cobwebs with giant spiders on them. I found a door and couldn't believe my eyes...

Ilona Noble (12)

Fraserburgh Academy, Fraserburgh

SCARY NIGHT

A group of friends went to a scary house and took a Ouija board. They put the board on the ground and put their two fingers on the check piece and said, "If there is a spirit with us, make yourself known now." The check piece moved around in circles and stopped.
They asked, "Are you good or bad?" It went to the moon symbol, so it was bad. They also asked how it died. It answered: 'lightning'. Then a bolt struck and they didn't say goodbye, so the spirit would haunt them forever.
The next day, they all died.

Alexander Wisely (13)
Fraserburgh Academy, Fraserburgh

THE CREEPIEST ADVENTURE

It was a dark, foggy night and I was outside of a tall, haunted castle. I was with my excited friends. We all went inside the haunted castle. The stairs were made of cracked concrete, it was not safe. When we opened the door, the door was creaking so loud you could hear it from like a mile away. We all stuck together in the mysterious, haunted, creepy castle. I saw a closet in the corner of the dark, spooky room. I whispered, "Who's opening it?"
A random voice replied, "Get out now, we see you!"
We ran so fast.

Jensen Strachan (12)
Fraserburgh Academy, Fraserburgh

THE TWINS

The train was abandoned. My arm hairs sprung up like a cat. As I slowly trembled up the steps, I felt an eerie presence looming over me. There was someone, no, something there. As I crept down the walkway, quick footsteps behind me were chasing me down.
Out of thin air, a tall, wide-shouldered man towered over me. His eyes were peeled back with metal machinery and he had a cackling laugh. I struggled to move back. After a couple of steps, I bumped into something. I felt scales caressing my back and nails scratching me. It was the twins...

Adam Boyd (13)
Fraserburgh Academy, Fraserburgh

THE HUNT BEGINS

She is pale and trembling like a leaf. She says, "Ben," in a faint voice. She is thrown into the dark doorway. Behind her, I scream, "Liz!" No response. I run into the dark doorway without thinking. It's cold with the smell of rotten flesh. Something with a cold and bony hand pulls me down. I try to crawl away but it's too powerful. I hear snarling as it comes into the little light. Its breath smells like a rotten carcass. I get a look at its hideous face as it edges closer, breathing heavier. Its hand on my face...

Ben McGruther (14)
Fraserburgh Academy, Fraserburgh

THE FUNFAIR

It was the night that the funfair came to town. I was there with my best friend Olivia. Everything was going well until all the rides broke down. There was a sudden loud screech and everything went black. I was confused, standing there shivering. The lights came back on but nobody was there, except a tall man with a clown mask on and a chainsaw. I ran as fast as I could before the man could get me. He yelled, "Stop!" Suddenly, I was unable to move. He slowly walked towards me and said, "It's your turn, choose wisely..."

Jennifer Smith (13)
Fraserburgh Academy, Fraserburgh

ONE NIGHT WHILE CAMPING

A mother told her son to get some water from the well that they saw while travelling up the mountain. When he didn't return, the mother began to get worried. She called the police and they organised a huge search party.
A week later, they still couldn't find the boy.
A day later, a hiker found him and gave him back to his family. Once he had returned, he explained that a tall, faceless man kidnapped him and took him to a cabin up in the mountain. The sheriff said that there'd never been a cabin up in the mountain...

Fraser Ross (13)
Fraserburgh Academy, Fraserburgh

THE FIGURE

I turned the corner and saw a tall, still figure looking around through the fog. I turned the next corner. *Flash!* Lightning struck and the figure was there, even closer. I could see the figure was seven-foot tall with extremely long arms. As it got closer, I could see more of the figure. This was no human. This was a creature, a monstrous creature.
Bang! The wind started to howl and the fog started to disappear. I wanted to run but I was frozen. *Bam!* I blinked and it was behind me, a chainsaw against my neck...

Isabella Traves (13)
Fraserburgh Academy, Fraserburgh

GHOST RUNNER

It was 2:30am. Josh was in his old Mustang driving down a dark, winding, desolate road coming back from somewhere that he should never have been. He was in the middle of nowhere. A storm was blowing in. The wind whistled, the rain fell and lightning struck. *Crash!* Lightning struck his car. He ran out and watched his car set alight. He felt like he was being watched by someone or something.
Just then, the trees began to fall in the wind. Amongst the trees lay a transparent being-like thing. It woke up and charged at him...

Israel Noble (12)
Fraserburgh Academy, Fraserburgh

THE OLD CASTLE

A door slammed behind me. My heart beat as fast as I could blink. Everything went black. *What do I do?* I was just going for a nice, peaceful walk, breathing in all the fresh air. Then I saw a very old, mysterious castle. The sky went really dull and grey, so I went closer and before I knew it, I was inside the big, mysterious castle. It smelt like there was rotting food lying somewhere inside. It was disgusting. I was looking around and then the door slammed. I saw the cupboard open and shut.
"Oh no!" I said...

Amy-Louise McDonnell (13)
Fraserburgh Academy, Fraserburgh

THE GRAVEYARD CREATURE

The dark, damp forest had an old church that was barely standing and an ancient graveyard that was at least 200 years old. Two teens thought it would be a good idea to go and spend the night in there.
As soon as they got there, James had a bad feeling about it, but Marc insisted that they stayed. James heard something scuttling through the graveyard. Then Marc felt a cold breath down his neck which made his hair stand on its end. A faint voice whispered, "Boys." Marc felt a drip of blood on his nose. Then it struck...

Luke Norrie (15)
Fraserburgh Academy, Fraserburgh

THE GRAVEYARD

It was a dark, stormy night. I was walking down the path next to the old graveyard when I heard a high-pitched scream. I stopped in fear. All the hairs on my arms stuck up like needles. I walked forwards into the graveyard. Again, I heard the scream. It was coming from the old church. I took a couple of steps forward. I stepped on a stick. *Snap!* I jumped. I walked into the church and the doors slammed behind me. "Hello?" I turned around slowly. I tried to open the door but it wouldn't open. Then I heard...

Glenn McDonald (13)
Fraserburgh Academy, Fraserburgh

THE SECRET OF MIDDLETOWN

The bells rang loudly. The night had begun. I was walking near a creepy church on Fell Road when I heard perishing screams and smelt burning corpses. I had heard the rumours in the town centre of the demons of the night but thought nothing of it. That's until I saw a body drained of blood in the middle of the sidewalk outside the church. When I took a photograph of the body, I noticed there was a tall, black, skinny figure in the background. At this point, my whole body was trembling because I knew that night brought death.

Mia Morrice (14)
Fraserburgh Academy, Fraserburgh

THE HAUNTED SHOP

At 3am, I was working in the shop. Then suddenly... *Boom!* A lightning bolt struck and the power went off. Then I heard a mysterious giggle. Was it just in my head? I went to turn the power back on. I opened the circuit board... *Bam!* Someone or something must have been in the shop. So I took a knife off the shelf and started to walk into the back to escape, but I heard the giggle again. I sprinted into the back, scared for my life. I kicked open the back door and then... *Splash!* Blood everywhere...

Logan King (12)
Fraserburgh Academy, Fraserburgh

DARKNESS

I think I lost it but it's too late to go back home. I glance up. There it is, the old, abandoned house. It's my only option. I sprint towards it and I'm facing the door. My cold, trembling hand reaches the old, crooked handle. I push the door open. I walk inside. It slams behind me - darkness. I pull out my phone - 10% - maybe enough for a phone call. I put on my phone's torch and look around. *Bang!* I turn around too quickly, shivers going down my spine. I drop my phone and the light goes out...

Leah Milton (14)
Fraserburgh Academy, Fraserburgh

THE ROTTEN HOSPITAL

It was Friday the 13th. My friend and I stumbled across an old hospital. It had been closed down because of a rat infestation problem a few years back. We started to approach the door. As we got to the door, this vile smell came from an open window on the ground floor. Liz was adamant that we shouldn't go in, but I didn't listen to her. We walked around the first floor and as soon as we turned the corner, there were 30 dead, rotten corpses. We were about to scream but then we heard the most awful sound...

Kirra Guild (13)

Fraserburgh Academy, Fraserburgh

THE HAUNTING OF EDINBURGH CASTLE

We finally reached the forbidden castle. We were scared. It was eerie. We moved to the upstairs of the house and came across a dog. He started barking, then disappeared into the night. We were petrified, so we ran to the front door. It slammed suddenly, so we ran to the cellar to find another way out. We had scratches and bruises all over our bodies. At the bottom of the cellar, it was empty except for a chair with a doll. It rose from the chair and started chasing us. "We need to get out of here right now!"

Kael Hay (13)

Fraserburgh Academy, Fraserburgh

THE BODY

I arrived at the scary, tall, creaky haunted house. I slowly walked through the door. The wind was blowing on my back. There wasn't a sight to be seen. I looked around and saw a black, wooden cupboard with cobwebs all over it. I went to open it. A body fell out with force onto the squeaky floor. Now I was shaking in terror. A window burst open. The wind shot inside. I ran as fast as I could up the stairs. Something was chasing me. It grabbed me. Everything went black. I don't think I'll escape this one...

Mya Brebner (13)
Fraserburgh Academy, Fraserburgh

NO ESCAPE

I grasped the rusty handle in the hope of finding shelter from the Baltic wind that rushed up my jacket, leaving a shiver on my spine. The door creaked open, leaving a small spider hanging from a cobweb attached to the rotten door frame. I stepped in. *Bang!* The door slammed shut on me. I reached for my bag, in search of my phone. No signal. I ran to an open window where the wind and rain hurled through and it suddenly slammed shut. What was I going to do? Was I the only living body in this creepy house?

Molly Poyser (13)
Fraserburgh Academy, Fraserburgh

THE ASYLUM

My head throbbed with a migraine as I walked back home in the rain. I was struggling to walk, losing the will to live. I looked around desperately for somewhere to rest when I saw a vintage-looking building. I ran up the wooden stairs to the door and turned the cold, metal handle. I looked in. There was an empty room, a staircase, fireplace and wooden chair. I stumbled over and sat down. I began to take in the details of the room and noticed a dead man on the staircase. Soon, I would be laid beside him, dead...

Niamh Evans (12)
Fraserburgh Academy, Fraserburgh

THE SPOOKY, DEEP CELLAR

I crept along the squeaky floorboards. A door opened. A ghost flew out and started chasing me. I ran until I couldn't run any further. I stopped and it flew straight through me. I screamed and ran. A passageway opened. I slid down and found myself in a deep, dark cellar. It was impossible to climb back up the steep, long, curvy slide. I found a door and opened it. It was the way out, so I ran along it and the ghost chased me. I was running along the long, curvy, deep corridor until the door slammed shut!

Brooke Drewett (12)
Fraserburgh Academy, Fraserburgh

A BUMP IN THE NIGHT

As I walked down the dusty, creaky, wooden floor, I wandered past the rooms I thought my friends were in. As I kept walking, I felt a chilling breeze. It pricked up the hair on the back of my neck. It was weird, it felt human, like it was trying to talk to me. I couldn't make out what it said, but my curiosity decided to follow it.
When I got down the cold, cracked, spiral staircase, it disappeared. The strange figure had gone, but then I heard it; the sound from the walls. The bump in the night...

Darren Dickie (14)
Fraserburgh Academy, Fraserburgh

THE ABANDONED HOUSE

I slowly put my shaky hand out to open the aged black door of the old, abandoned house. As soon as I touched the door, a shiver shot down my body. There was a loud creak as it opened. It was dark and eerie and we only had one torch with us which was starting to flicker. There were spiderwebs everywhere. The wallpaper was hanging off the walls and there were holes in the floor. We clambered upstairs. Something felt off upstairs. We were standing in the middle of this bedroom when suddenly, it went dark...

Danny Davidson (14)
Fraserburgh Academy, Fraserburgh

THE PARTY

Me and my friends were at a house party. We were all a bit drunk and decided to get out a Ouija board. As we were getting it out, I heard a bang coming from upstairs. I went to check it out. I looked in the bathroom and the shower curtain was closed. I reached for the curtain and pulled it. Nothing was there, so I went back downstairs to the basement. Everyone was lying there with holes in their heads. It looked like they'd been drilled. There were also holes ripped into their chests. He had come...

Keiran Duncan (12)
Fraserburgh Academy, Fraserburgh

THE TUNNEL

As I walked across the overgrown path, I caught my foot in a spiky plant. I stumbled to the ground and something unexpected happened. As I sat on the ground, the path opened to reveal a gloomy, dark tunnel. I was shaking like a leaf and my heart was beating like a drum. What should I do? Go down the tunnel or run home as fast as possible?
I finally made my decision, closed my eyes and took a leap of faith. I could feel the gravity pushing me down. I finally came to a stop and was shivering cold...

Isobel Short (13)
Fraserburgh Academy, Fraserburgh

TRAPPED

Her face became pale. She stood in front of the metal doors and gulped with fright as she slowly reached for the handle. The door creaked as she opened it. Her eyes opened wildly and her cold sweat dripped down her. It was hard for her to process what she saw, but as she began to walk in, she heard the door close behind her. "What the-" she said. As she turned to look, her vision went blurry. Her chest started to hurt, but why? She had no idea what caused it. Then she dropped to the ground...

Lilly Frandzelska
Fraserburgh Academy, Fraserburgh

THE ESCAPE

He was chasing her along the corridor with laughter that sent shivers down her spine. His knife was sharp with blood dripping down it. Was she going to be his next victim? As she sped up, she could see the sun starting to rise. She was going to be safe, she was going to survive! Or so she thought. As she burst out the door with the man slightly behind her, she could feel the warm sun on her skin. She didn't care if blood was dripping down her arm as she was already dead. There was no escaping him.

Zofia Dramska (13)
Fraserburgh Academy, Fraserburgh

THE CREEPY CASTLE

I tried to move around the castle, then fell down a humongous hole. It took me down to the basement. Something tugged my arm. I felt scared. It was pitch-black. I couldn't see a thing. I tried to feel for a door. Once I'd found it, it took me back outside. It was daylight again. The castle was ginormous and dark. Its colours were black and grey. I went back in and when I entered, the lights came on and it was pink and white. The carpets were red with spilt blood. The bodies were torn open...

Imogen Strachan (13)
Fraserburgh Academy, Fraserburgh

THE CREEPY MANSION

It was the scariest day of my life. About two weeks ago, I received an eerie phone call. It was from a 'No Caller ID' telling me to go to an old mansion near my house. The caller was an old man with a terrifying laugh. He hung up as soon as I asked him for his name.
I arrived at the mansion and opened the old, wrecked door. I went up the long staircase and a flash of lightning struck right outside. The door slammed shut. The last thing I remember is getting chased out of the door...

Owen Pearson (12)
Fraserburgh Academy, Fraserburgh

THE KIDNAPPING

I woke up tied to a chair with my mouth covered. I looked around in wonder. Where were my friends? Where was I? I managed to untie myself and got up to look around. I heard a scream and ran to the door to try and open it, but it was locked. The screams got louder and louder. I realised there was a body. It was mine. I was dead. The screams were mine. I just realised that although the screams were mine, they sounded like someone else's. Even though I was dead, I didn't feel it, or was I?

Millie Duthie (13)
Fraserburgh Academy, Fraserburgh

ARSON

You wake and roll over in what you think is your bed, but as you open your eyes, you begin to realise that this is definitely not your bed, or house for that matter. You get out of the bed, only to trip and bump into the table, causing a vase holding a withered rose to fall off and shatter on the floor. Out of instinct, you sprint over to the wardrobe in the corner of the room and hide in it. You hear footsteps coming your way. The handle of the door shakes for a moment...
Then nothing.

Rebecca Daniel (12)
Fraserburgh Academy, Fraserburgh

MISDIRECTED

As I was walking home from work, I saw a sign that said my address. *Shortcut?* I came across this old, abandoned building. It looked very run-down with holes in the roof and boarded up windows. I had some time to kill, so I walked up to the house. I started to hear the pitter-patter of rain and I had a bad feeling in my gut. I entered and I was greeted by a big, mouldy staircase. I walked up the stairs and heard a big, massive thud in the next room. Who could it be? A monster?

Charlie Buchan (14)
Fraserburgh Academy, Fraserburgh

THE SPIDERS INVADE

I slowly reached out my hand and turned the door handle to open the door. Behind the door, loads of spiders started crawling out, so I screamed at the top of my voice and ran. I forgot to close the door. Loads of spiders were chasing after me. Behind all the spiders, there was a button. I grabbed a ladder and climbed up. I was shaking as the spiders got closer and closer. As they climbed up the ladder, I jumped. I ran as fast as I could. I shut the door and pressed the red button...

Lola Mitchell (12)
Fraserburgh Academy, Fraserburgh

THE FUNFAIR

We went to the annual funfair that came to town. We had just come off The Spinner, a really fast ride, when I spotted a funhouse with a clown's face for a door. It was new. The others were still feeling sick from The Spinner, so I went in by myself. I regret that now. It was almost pitch-black except for a small, dim light on the floor. I looked at all the mirrors. They were funny. One made me tall, another made me small. The last one had a clown. Wait, it was a real clown...

Eilidh Meadows (12)
Fraserburgh Academy, Fraserburgh

THE HAUNTING

It was a Sunday night and we had to get back early because we had school tomorrow, so when we were on our way home, we decided to take the shortcut. I was with my five best friends. On the way, we found an abandoned house and we went in. *Bang!* Something fell from the ceiling. We took a step back. Something was moving in the pile of dust but we couldn't quite make out what it was. I went over to have a look when it turned around and jumped on me...

Theo Watt (12)
Fraserburgh Academy, Fraserburgh

A SPOOKY NIGHT

One day on a very creepy night I went to a castle to explore it, then I heard a door bang. It could have been a draft. The place was old, like really old and it was supposed to be haunted. Then a couple of hours later I heard a voice saying, "Come here." I started to freak out so I tried to run out of the room and then the door slammed shut. So I had to run out of the other door. I made it out the front door and went home.

Billy Whyte (12)
Fraserburgh Academy, Fraserburgh

THE SMELL OF FEAR

I walked in. There was a vile smell that reminded me of some sort of gas. It suddenly went black. I felt like I was floating. I heard a scream, a high-pitched scream. I felt my heart beat faster as my vision came back. I was no longer feeling the floating sensation as a strange figure emerged from around the corner. Before I could wriggle free, he was standing over me...

Kaleb Gibson (13)

Fraserburgh Academy, Fraserburgh

THE SHADOWS ARE NEAR

Fog was creeping in. I wouldn't make it back before dark. I saw an old church. *I'll wait there and call Mot*, I thought. Fog weaved around the weather-beaten tombs. I shivered. I crept between crumbling gravestones, heading for the church. The door latch was rusty but unlocked. I entered and shut the door behind me. "Hello?" No answer.
I called Mot. "I'll be there in twenty, Zil!" he said. I sat on a dusty pew. Moonlight cast dark shadows through the stained glass windows. *Bang!*
"Mot?" The shadows, still moving, grew bigger. A cold hand touched my shoulder. "Mot?"

Aaron Whitby (14)
Frome College, Frome

WHAT I DID TO YOU

"Pain," says the voice. "Pain." One. Two. Three. Four. My heartbeat counts back the years, unwanted recollections invading my mind in countless waves of bitter repentance. I open my eyes and she's there with her blank eyes, delicate frown and clothes of mist.
"Look what you did to me," she whispers. Blood chokes from my lungs in laboured gasps, terror breaking a cold sweat across my brow, desperation clouding the world in violent red. She digs her nails into my flesh, blood erupting from the wounds, burning the tears, replacing them with flames.
"You're supposed to be dead."

Amaya Murguialday (14)
Frome College, Frome

EMPTY

She has no face. Black as night, a wedding dress surrounds her emptiness. She doesn't move, only stares. Somehow, she's still, frozen in time, despite the evening winds. Staring into your frostbitten soul. You don't know she's there; she only comes when you're sleeping. You wake up from the melody of the chirping birds but you look out your window and they're dead. Lifeless. You've heard of the old witch tales involving departed birds. Weirdly, this is different. Something is wrong, but you need sleep, so you turn around to your bed and she's there. Agnes has come for you...

Ashley Gahagan (15)
Frome College, Frome

THE VANISHING ACT

Last lesson of the day. Just one more lesson until I was free for the summer. As I was walking, something started flickering. Just a little at first. Just the lights. But no, the people were flickering too. Then just like that, gone. Everyone gone. Then it appeared. The fear I felt at that moment was unparalleled. Then nothing.
Andrew walked into school after the summer and spotting his friends, ran over to them. Scanning their faces, he asked, "Has anyone seen Josh?" Apparently, they hadn't. That chatted casually until the bell went. When the bell went, the world started flickering...

Oliver Marshall (15)
Frome College, Frome

EVVLE CAVE

In Evvle forest laid a cave, its roof reached out like an arm grasping food. A few metres inside, the slimy floor dropped, sinking never-endingly into a pitch-black abyss thousands of kilometres deep. Looking over the edge, there was an endless hanging larder of grimy bodies hanging from green ropes of mucus. One of the meals snapped its head sideways and screeched, "Here it comes!" It laughed hysterically. Suddenly, a huge, grey, worm-like beast leapt up and a new silhouette appeared on the ceiling to hang eternally, never dying, slowly rotting, in constant pain and fear of the slimy monster.

Matthew Willis (15)
Frome College, Frome

BEHIND THE DOOR...

Emily's fingers closed around the varnished oak door handle. Gripping as hard as she could, as if it was her most precious possession, like an old childhood toy. Full of life, full of love, but this had never felt love. It was cold to touch, empty, filling her with resentment with every passing second. And yet, she would not let it go. She needed to see what was in the room beyond. It was pulling her in. The doorknob started turning. *Pulling*. The door creaked open just enough to see inside. *Pulling*. "Hello?" Emily whispered. "Hello again, Emily..."

Lola Francomb (14)
Frome College, Frome

PREDATOR

My coarse skin peels against my cracked ribs as I lie upon the forest floor littered with residues of nature and blood. The night pools around me, peaceful shades of eternal death. An arid breath caresses my cheek. I know his eyes of muskwood which obtain no flicker of prevailing emotion; only unfathomable cruelty. They crease as his lips curve upwards sinisterly, not unlike a wolf. One examines me for vulnerability. His skeletal hands graze my forehead, his wolfish lips on my ribs. Delicate until I shudder. His teeth strike - puncturing lungs. My father's name withering on my tongue...

Connie Bates (15)
Frome College, Frome

FOOTSTEPS

Thump, thump, thump. My heart was like a heavy drum travelling through my entire body. My breath came out in loud exhales. *Could he hear me? No, keep running. Just keep running.* The twigs and mud crunched beneath my bare feet as they ran across the marshy, sludgy ground. I couldn't breathe. I needed to stop. I crumbled to the ground, breathing heavily from exhaustion, my nightdress smothered in blood. I couldn't believe it, I had escaped! I was free. Wait, what was that? *Crunch.* Footsteps. Oh no...
I screamed as he held his hand over my mouth...

Polly Lynn (14)
Frome College, Frome

THE ARSONIST

Candle wax dripped heavily from the unattended candle. Falling carelessly onto the carpet, sparks turned into flames, travelling across the floor and up the beams. Smoke sat in the air, smothering the inhabitants who fell to the floor one by one like snowflakes. Flames soon engulfed the house, destroying what once seemed so permanent. Frames smashed, cabinets burned, bodies were cremated... Sirens in the distance were bells of death. He stood outside the house, the corner of his mouth turned up into a smirk. He placed the matches back in his pocket and moved on to the next house...

Lola Cox (14)
Frome College, Frome

HAVE I BEEN HERE BEFORE?

Drip, drip, drip; walking down the ominous corridor. That's all I could hear until a scream broke the silence. Walking faster now, the lights started flickering. I looked out of the window - thunder was rolling in. The lights cut out. *It's fine*, I thought. I had a torch. Slowly, I reached into my backpack to get it out. It was dead. I continued on with my journey down the dark, gloomy corridor. A cold shiver went down my spine. I looked behind me - nothing. I started walking faster. I felt a cold hand grab my shoulder. I turned around, screaming...

Toby Evans (15)
Frome College, Frome

RAILWAY MYSTERY

It was a bright, sunny day. The railway station was crowded but no trains were coming. The train commander came out and everyone gathered around. Suddenly, the doors were creaking and the wind was going crazy. There was a loud crash. Just like that, the commander was gone.
Within seconds, people started dropping onto the floor, even onto the tracks. Just five were left on the platform. Broken mirrors began scattering down. Some of the mirrors landed on the fallen. They got up and began walking uncontrollably. There was a scraping at the windows but nobody was there.

Natalie Latham (14)
Frome College, Frome

THE HAUNTED

Harsh laughter echoed through the woods, followed by hacking coughs as clouds of smoke billowed from the teenagers gathered around the bleeding badger. Trees swayed as a gust of wind knotted their hair. As the laughter died down, the four of them noticed the crunching of leaves. Turning to look, they didn't notice the disappearance of one until they heard a scream. The confidence from earlier, long gone. Slowly, one by one, a scream left their lips until just one was left. Turning to look behind her as she felt the feeling of being watched, it was her turn now...

Caitlin Roche (14)
Frome College, Frome

DARKNESS

Black, black and more black. It goes on forever, this darkness. I feel lost and alone in the forgotten depths of a hollow planet. I wish I had something other than the sound of my shuffling footsteps to accompany me. But... there is something. A faint rustling and shuffling that perhaps isn't my feet. Definitely isn't my feet. Not my breath, clothes, or me at all. I'm realising how oppressive this darkness is, the way it clings to my clothes, seeps into the very fibres of my being. The sickly cloying sensation of being suffocated by the lack of light...

Lilith Whitelaw (15)
Frome College, Frome

THE HAUNTED

Blood dripped warmly down the side of his face, diluting the bathwater to a cold pink colour. His vision went fuzzy as a stretched face loomed over him. Coldness poured over his skin, the bathwater now overflowing. The face moved and shifted to settle into a freakishly human expression; eyes glowing and mouth wide, skin peeling away and falling to the edge of his vision. Suddenly, it let out a silent screech, ear-splittingly quiet. The ringing that followed was surely enough to drive any living man insane. The noise was forever captured in the poor man's ears.

Juno Mclachlan (14)
Frome College, Frome

THE GHOST

Above me, crows were creating a cacophony of noise as I slowly turned the handle. The door creaked open. Stepping inside, shivers crept down my spine and raised the hairs on the back of my neck. Something told me I shouldn't be there, that I didn't belong. Shoving the fear deep inside, I continued into the room, half-hidden by shadows. Empty, apart from a stone fireplace. A feeling that I was being watched rose from the darkness. I turned around and froze. A pearly white, transparent figure was hovering in the doorway. A scream escaped from my mouth...

Daniella Backhurst (15)
Frome College, Frome

PUNCHBAG

Trapped. The air heavy, my breaths slow and deep. I heard a door open. Footsteps getting closer, getting louder. Coughing, I tried to catch my breath between the punches. One after the other. Punch after punch. Something trickled down my face, the darkness disguising its colour. Blood. The pain was excruciating. The swaying was giving me motion sickness. Everything went still, silent. Two hands rested on the other side of the fabric. My breaths were the same slow pace as theirs. The sound of metal escaping a plastic case sliced the air. Then it sliced me...

Maya Barlow (13)
Frome College, Frome

A DREAM NOT TO BE FORGOTTEN

Astonishment relieved the anticipating mind of the wanted. Clouds broke over the spires that crawled into the night. I stumbled up the dew-soaked hill with a screaming gust pushing my thoughts aside. *It's okay*, beckoned the wind's call. I was drawn like a moth to a flickering lamp, a magnet to metal, me to danger. I entered the threshold. Torches threw my shadow against the dark, mossy, stone cold wall. I stared up just to catch the fleeting eye. My mind whirled, my body swirled and I screamed as my mind erupted out of a sweat-soaked dream.

Elwood Garrett (14)
Frome College, Frome

OUR SECRET

Every day, I'd return home to nothing out of the ordinary. Everything in its place, an equilibrium of my own. But soon enough, things started to move and change. From small objects moving out of place, to dark crimson liquid spilt upon my floor and counter. Some days were worse than others. I never called the police, nor a friend. A stench had built up from my basement. What a shame. My friends and family lay in a similar pool of red liquid.
Unfortunately, since you now know my secret, you shall be joining them. I'll see you soon, my friend...

Patrycja Raczkowska (15)
Frome College, Frome

THE HOUSE OF DEMONS

The mist was crawling. The boy, no older than you or me, wasn't going to make it home before nightfall. An old house loomed into view over the fields in the distance. The boy decided that he'd seek refuge there for the night. The mist encased the lonely house, the natural stone was chilling to the touch. No candles were lit in the house. He knocked on the door. *Bang! Bang!* No answer. Then the door opened. From the dim light, a faint figure disappeared from view. No noise, no gestures. He stepped inside. The door slammed shut behind him...

William Payne (15)
Frome College, Frome

BURNING

Bang! Bang! Bang! I heard footsteps upstairs. It must have followed me. The thuds were getting closer and closer. Seconds later, a huge, indescribable shadow was crawling down the wall as a horrifying, burnt-looking figure followed. Then suddenly, the house lit up into an inferno. The searing pain of the flames engulfing my entire body was taken over by the feeling of smoke filling my lungs, suffocating me as I reached for breath. Then those smoky claws that were grasping onto my lungs, finally let go. It was completely dark and peaceful...

Alisha Ali-Davey (14)
Frome College, Frome

THE COLD HAND

The red, blazing sun sets over the abandoned house. The roaring wind batters the house, torturing the tired windows on their rusty hinges. Inside, there are many ancient pictures of people staring through my soul, their eyes stalking me as I creep past. A large immaculate mirror stands proud in the upstairs bedroom. I glance into the mirror. A figure towers behind me. I can feel a cold hand clench onto my shoulder. I look behind but nothing is there. The cold hand grips onto me tighter. I look into the pristine mirror but I am no longer standing there...

Hayden Pepler (14)
Frome College, Frome

THE PRISONER

The deep, dark depths of my mind wither and shrink as the horror of my terrifying position undulates in and out of my malnourished brain. The bright strikes of lightning arc across the sky, searing bright, white light into the retinas of my unaccustomed eyes. The dust, once settled, now disturbed, swirls, twirls, skims and slides around my feet and legs. The silence screams in my ears. Pound after pound, slam after slam sound against the inside of my skull, like a starving prisoner asking, begging, pleading to be released and now I have been released.

Gethin Henley (15)
Frome College, Frome

BUTTONS

Ever since we'd moved, something had always been throwing buttons around. At first, I thought it was my wife. I let her get away with it as a joke. That changed when she came to me saying, "Stop throwing buttons at me!" Buttons were left around our apartment. All black buttons. What pushed us over the edge was when there was a trail of bloody red buttons heading to the locked door. The whole room was covered in buttons. In the room, there was a dead child no older than five. Sewn into its eyes were the same bloody red buttons...

Frankie Patterson (14)
Frome College, Frome

THE CASTLE PLAN

Once there was a girl. She came across a castle that was being renovated. She walked inside but didn't realise it was haunted. She went to leave but the door was shut. She tried to escape but she couldn't. Then she heard whispering. She followed the sound. It led her to a door. She walked inside and spotted some children. She smiled and asked if she could play with them. They agreed and allowed her to play. After a while, she stopped and smiled at them. When she looked again, they were gone.
A few minutes later, they killed her.

Paige Seymour (15)
Frome College, Frome

MOTHER

The white clouds, now tainted grey, hung above the cottage. I hadn't been to my mother's house since her death, but I had a job to do.
Entering the dimly lit cottage, I was greeted with an overwhelming cold rush that swept over my brittle body. The atmosphere was eerie, unwelcoming. The mirror in the corner of the room reflected a tired and insipid figure - at first, I felt comforted as it held the resemblance of my mother. Until the eyes grew a crimson colour as the figure darkened and its mouth fell agape. This was not my mother.

Ella Breese (17)
Frome College, Frome

TAKEN

The creepy hooting of the owls ahead, the spine-chilling breeze, the occasional broken stick under small feet. It was all scary for a ten-year-old girl. Especially in the woods at midnight, far enough from anyone so that no one would be able to hear her scream.
After walking for a while, getting cold and tired, the girl began to run. She'd heard a blood-curdling scream behind her and felt a chilling presence. She ran until she felt safe. But then a woman dressed in all white suddenly appeared and took her away, never to be seen again.

Ro Butler (15)
Frome College, Frome

THEY WERE RIGHT

The rattle of thunder echoes through my bones as I scramble to my feet, rain trickling down my back, a shiver running down my frozen spine. The stories were true: graveyards are dangerous at night. The labyrinth of old gravestones encircles me until I come to a halt, gazing upon one in particular. I'm not alone. I saunter to the stone, each step further into the muddy earth until I'm standing in front of it. The tightening of a noose catches my breath, heaving my legs off the floor. They were right: graveyards are dangerous at night.

Liliana Burbidge (14)
Frome College, Frome

TICKING

The moonbeams fell gently through the open window as Simon lay awake, listening to the ominous ticking of the clock in the hall. He didn't know how long he'd been there, alone in that old house. But before long, the clock began to chime. Once, twice until twelve times, filling the night with its noise. Once it had stopped, Simon rolled over to face the door. It flew open with a shattering crash. Through the opening, stepped a ghostly figure. It turned to face him and opened its gap-toothed jaw into a horrifying, piercing scream...

Morgan Abram-Maggs (14)
Frome College, Frome

THE SPIRIT IN THE MIRROR

I was alone, just me and the spirit in the mirror. It weirdly resembled me; matted black hair, dark clothes. It stared at me as I sat on my floor trying to figure out what it was. It started to talk, a familiar voice. "You will kill someone tonight," it whispered, a haunting message. I began to panic. *I'm killing someone?*
Hours of fear and panic passed. I grabbed a knife from the kitchen and dug it into my victim. However, I was still alone. I was my own victim. That faceless spirit... I knew it had my scars.

Katie Bond (14)
Frome College, Frome

LET ME OUT

I stumble through these putrid, bloody hospital corridors; screams of pain and hatred echoing down the halls. Doors open to people strapped to hospital beds, these patients being injected with horrifying chemicals. I stumble further, the pain in my head increasing as I reach the gate at the end of the corridor. I go faster and faster and faster until I explode into the way out at the end of the vile hallway. It is a whitish, yellow padded cell with no way out. I stare at the horror in the centre, unable to calm the terror. It's me.

Callum Shaw (14)
Frome College, Frome

THE MONSTERS BENEATH

As I enter the flooded caves looking for the wreckage and any survivors, there's seismic activity at the entrance to the caves. The tunnels look like they're some kind of hive. As I descend deeper into the tunnels, I can hear clicking sounds as my oxygen tank is about to run out. I find a large air bubble, but I can still hear the clicking. Something moves. The clicks turn into a high-pitched screech as a horde of spider-like creatures appears, with a family car-sized one leading them. There is no hope. It's the end for me.

Jimmie Webb (14)
Frome College, Frome

SHARDS OF ENERGY: THE BEAST

Crash! The plate slid off the table onto the hard, chiselled floor. Quickly, I rushed into the room to view what caused it to smash. Silence. Rain cascaded down past the tinted windows beside me as I explored my surroundings. Suddenly, a figure appeared. Great and ghastly, filled with anger and fury. I dashed out of the door in an attempt to escape as it leapt in my direction. Panicking, I grabbed a knife, hoping it could save me from the beast. I turned and went for the kill with my final shards of energy. It was over for me.

Rory Berry (15)
Frome College, Frome

ETERNITY

He is dying, but it is okay. The black-red blossoms out, growing, twisting, staining. The face of his partner watches his eyes; he lets his gaze fall past the gun and onto her face. Mirrored, reflected, identical. She isn't surprised at the knife in her chest. He isn't surprised at the bullet in his. Together forever, for eternity. He calls her name. She calls his. They smile as they fall. Together forever, for eternity. She holds the baby to her heart. He takes it from her and they walk away. Together forever, for eternity.

Edie Ray (14)
Frome College, Frome

MISTAKES

I think it all started one day in spring. But if I'm completely honest, it could have been summer. I remember the blazing heat because I'd taken off my blazer and I'd spent the entirety of the day pulling up my socks. My first mistake that day was taking the longer path through the woods. The second was dismissing my paranoia as social anxiety. It was a couple of steps past the largest tree that I saw her bag. She was someone I remembered walking home with from time to time. However, she was dead, and now, so was I.

Ann Mota (15)

Frome College, Frome

THE PUPPET MASTER

It started off with mice for his tea party. Then doves, sheep, baby bears. The options were limitless for him. If he wanted a friend, I would find one for him. Soon, he wanted more than an animal friend, so I found him a real friend. His name was Tom Rogan. He was a nice boy, son of the Rogan couple who pulled the strings of the town. But now I'm the one pulling their son's strings like a puppeteer for my brother's tea party. His lifeless limbs pouring tea for my little brother, while I pull his puppet strings...

Titus Beaven (14)
Frome College, Frome

THE HOUSE OF DISENCHANTMENT

I stared at the hollowed carcass of a building. Its old, cladded walls whispered stories of curious children and foolish adults. Yet another person missing, but this time it was my job to figure it all out. I stood by the front gate, a stretch of withering grass lying between me and my fate. The glaring windows drew me in like a moth to a flame with their fragmented beauty. Chewing down on my fears, I walked up slowly to feel the cool touch of the wooden door on my shivering hands, and then I realised... I was already dead.

Owen White (17)
Frome College, Frome

IDYLL

I stand in an idyllic country lane. Birds chirp and tweet. The sky is the brightest blue hue I have ever seen. Nothing is wrong. Yet, everything is. I don't know how I got here. I don't know who I am. The sky darkens. That hue of brightest blue is overshadowed by the darkness. That darkness moves towards me. It tries to engulf me. The birdsong is gone, replaced by the creaking of the birds' skeletons. Realisation hits. This darkness comes from me. If only I could be happy, it would be fine. I cannot. Who am I?

Isabel Turner (14)
Frome College, Frome

THE HOODED FIGURE

Ben was alone in his school. It was dark, but it was only 3 o'clock - why was it so dark? Strangely, it was also warm and stormy. He strolled around his school but no one was there. The gates were locked. It wasn't normally like this. As he wandered to the gym, he passed an open door. It was then that he saw a... Ghost!
"Get out of here! He'll get you!" it warned. Ben looked around and saw a figure in a black hood moving towards him. He ran and ran but would never escape the shadow chasing him.

McKenzie Kelloway (14)
Frome College, Frome

THE MISSED TRAIN

I was running to try and catch the last train at 12:00am. It was getting very dark and very scary. As the night went on, strange things started to happen like whistling wind coming from all different directions. As I turned around to see if another train was coming, a weird shadow appeared behind me. Suddenly, flashing, bright lights came towards me. I thought to myself, *I hope it's the train coming*. It was getting very scary. I turned around with chills going down my spine and sweat dripping down my face...

Ella Maidment (14)
Frome College, Frome

THE JOURNEY

Going through the forest, no turns, just straight into the gloomy fog, not knowing what comes after. Looking around, I see ancient trees surrounding me. No sign of other life apart from leaves rotting on the floor. It's quite scary, the Unknown. You don't know what could happen next. I could be being watched by a man in a mask that is known for sinful ways in the next town over. The feeling of: could he be there? Could he be after me? What if? frightens me. Who, what is that? Is it him? Or am I making up things?

Freya Adriana (14)
Frome College, Frome

JILTED

His calm, sea-blue eyes staring into mine, he was just so perfect. We talked for hours that night. Just us. His smile that made me muddle my words sticks in my brain like a horror film. Such a shame I'll never see it again. Shame he chose her. We drank fine wine that night. He didn't enjoy it though. It was made from his blood. The screams he made will fuel my nightmares forever. If only he loved me, he wouldn't be six feet under. I mean, if I can't have him, no one can. I promise I'm not crazy...

Maisy Paton (14)
Frome College, Frome

GRANNY

Granny isn't dead. I am sure of it. She was a cruel, twisted lady who had made it her mission to make me suffer. So when Mum came and sat on my bed a few nights ago, I knew something had happened. I mourned the old hag for a while, but when her funeral came, I swear her chest moved. That's why I'm lying awake, listening for the smallest sound. "Tim!" I sit up dead straight. A shiver crawls up my spine. My eyes roam the room until they catch her eyes. I scream in terror and she smiles slightly...

Piper Watkins (14)
Frome College, Frome

THE CRUSADE OF BLOOD ROSES

The date was September 27th, 1886 when my dear sister was killed. I laid on her coffin a crusade of roses that carried the blood of my enemies. It dripped from them. It was too much to bear.
I awoke one day, a disoriented girl sitting on my bed, crying for my love. She stared into my soul and reached for the rope upon her legs. She whispered in my ear, "This is the mercy you wished for, brother." I stood up, her staring as she tied the noose around my neck. As she disappeared, I took my last breath...

Dean Baulf (15)
Frome College, Frome

YOU CAN NEVER KNOW WHAT'S IN THE DARK

The floorboard creaked, echoing throughout the house. Damn. As he relieved the pressure from the rotten wood, he saw a blurred figure in the cracked mirror in front of him. He turned from the mirror as stiff as a table leg, but when his eyes adjusted to the darkness, all he could see were the dusty clothes of the previous family. He had to get his prayers in now; it was suicide going in there. There was no escape if it had already seen you. His brother, the one he came here to save, was gone. He was already dead.

Addy Franklin-Turner (14)
Frome College, Frome

FEAR

It was a dark night in a small town called Shadesville. There was a house in the town with a family of four; a mother, father, son and daughter. At first, the family believed it was a normal day in Shadesville.
But that night, they were relaxing downstairs on the sofa when they heard a thud on the floor above them. They didn't think much of it until it happened again - and again! They started to worry and decided to check it out. As their dad started climbing the stairs, he slipped on some blood...

Nate Phelps (15)
Frome College, Frome

THE DARKNESS

It was just standing there. The dark figure's eyes were fire-red and they locked onto me. Its gaze was piercing and I couldn't run. I was bound there by fear. As it stared at me, I examined its long, slender body. Its fingers were long and sharp. It was tall and slim. It had no face other than the two eyes looking into my soul. I blinked once and it was gone. I was no longer stuck and I could move again. As fast as I could, I ran out of the building and I looked around...
It was there.

William Ibbitson (14)
Frome College, Frome

GONE

I had to walk home today. I was walking really fast, which is unusual as I normally walk slowly, but for some reason, I felt I had to. A shiver went down my back. There was one area of my journey that I didn't like. It was a small alleyway, but at the end of it was my house. As I was walking through it, a figure sprinted past me. I didn't think anything of it until I'd almost reached the end when another shadow ran by - except, when I stepped out of the alley, there was no one there...

Billy Haberfield (13)
Frome College, Frome

THE WINDOW

I was alone in my room. Suddenly, I heard a banging noise at my window. I thought it was just the wind, so I left it alone. But it kept persisting, so I went to the window. I saw a faceless man crouched by the window. Every sense left my body. I locked the window and ran. I called the police but they said that they couldn't find any trace of him.
Later that week, I was watching the news and that's when the same man appeared. He was reported to be a murderer. I was happy to be alive.

Daisy Bainton (14)
Frome College, Frome

THE STONY, GREY HAND

I felt it wrap around my ankle as I ran, pulling me down, further and further down. I didn't want to look. I really, really didn't want to look. Then I did... I let out a scream, a scream louder than I knew my voice could go. It was a stony, grey hand. I knew it would be. Why else would I be running? But I hadn't seen it and it didn't seem real until I did. I was still screaming. I was screaming until I couldn't anymore, until the dirt filled my lungs and the darkness came.

Tom Kelly (15)
Frome College, Frome

NEVER VISIT THE GRAVEYARD AT NIGHT

Lucy was at the graveyard visiting her mum's grave. It was midnight and it was foggy. The owls were her only company. She left the graveyard, hoping there was a taxi waiting. She heard her name. She looked around and there was a little girl. Lucy was terrified. She was as still as a statue. Suddenly, she started running until she got near a cliff. The girl kept calling her name. "Lucy, Lucy, Lucy..." Suddenly, she stopped because she was at the edge of the cliff. Would she jump?

Lilly Halfon (14)
Frome College, Frome

THE MYSTERIOUS FIGURE

Rose, a timid girl just 9 years of age, was in the middle of her large bedroom playing with a small doll she'd found in her toy box. She lifted the perfect, little doll up to the window to let her see the garden. It was then that she saw a dark, human figure standing outside looking up at her window. She darted to her covers to hide.
Minutes later, the figure flashed past her door. Her eyes locked onto it and she sat there stuck, frightened... The only thing she could do was scream.

Tom Wright (14)
Frome College, Frome

PARTY AT MIDNIGHT TAKES A TURN

I was at a party. There was loud music and fruit punch. Everyone was having fun. It was nearly midnight. People were dancing. There was this boy. He kept looking at me. He followed me around the room. I finally got the courage to talk to him. We talked for ages. Then I got a call from my dad describing someone who was very dangerous. It turned out it was the boy I'd been talking to all night. I was in the car with him. I noticed he was driving fast. I saw a gun and a knife. He stopped...

Georgia Litterick (14)
Frome College, Frome

THE CABIN

"Help!" shouted Liam. Soon, I followed. We had got lost in the Alaskan forest somehow. We had been walking for ages. Soon, we found a cabin and were welcomed by a man who let us stay the night.
When we woke up, we started looking for food in the attic where we found three bodies: two girls and a lady. We found a truck out in the back and drove away whilst phoning the police. However, the person who answered was the man. He said he would kill us both if we ever told anyone.

Oliver Dredge (14)
Frome College, Frome

NO ESCAPE

Breathing heavily, I kept running despite the heavy wind and rain feeling like flames on my bare skin. My heart pounded heavily. An alleyway, lit by only one dimly flickering street light encaptured with darkness. I sank to the floor, praying I was safe and that's when I saw them. A pair of feverish, scarlet eyes glaring ravenously at me. Unable to move, I sat there dazed and disorientated like a deer in headlights. Realisation hit me like a bullet, there was no escape...

Evie Lambourne (14)
Frome College, Frome

THE LAST STOP

I was cold. The train station was empty, abandoned almost. The ivy wrapped around my feet, too stubborn to let go. The train arrived. Broken windows, broken doors... Human-like figures, yet too translucent to be real, stepped off the train. Blood and tears poured down their faces. I took a glimpse at each one, knowing it was their last stop. They left peacefully. I got onto the train and looked down at my own translucent body, knowing that this would also be my last stop.

Shannon O'Connor (14)
Frome College, Frome

BALL PIT

It was a regular day shift. Families talked and children played in the ball pit. I took a particular liking to this family with twins. They always treated me well and the twins were both very charming. However, it was eventually time for them to go. They called, "Alex an-"
"Joshua?" I finished for them, wondering why they didn't call both of them.
"Who's Joshua?" they asked as if puzzled by the name.
"Yes, Joshua," I replied.
"We don't have another son," they stated, freaked out.
After that situation, I went to clean the ball pit. I found a finger...

Lennon Valkai (14)
Our Lady & St Bede Catholic Academy, Stockton-On-Tees

LOVESICK

Heavy breathing. Sprinting. Running. I couldn't bear the thought of looking back, seeing him. No, this thing, it wasn't human. At least, it didn't deserve to be. Not after what it'd done to me. This 'creature' was devoid of any emotions. Empty. Selfish. Only doing something for its own benefit; claiming it was 'ours'. "Dang it!" My legs felt numb, begging for me to stop, but I'd been running for so long. Now wasn't the time to give up. Exhausted, I tripped, landing on the muddy forest floor. "Damn!" I looked around, hearing an eerie whisper. "Found you, my love."

Laura Konopka (14)

Our Lady & St Bede Catholic Academy, Stockton-On-Tees

THE REALITY

This is a contest, right? About creepy events and gloomy scenes with hints of suspension and horror? Good, because I don't like writing about happy places, beaming children in flowering fields boasting about a perfect life because that's not the way life goes. Life itself is a brutal horror story; the swings and roundabouts are made only by humanity's stupidities. I wish I was wrong, honestly. But really, the only thing I'm scared of is losing everything I have grown to know and love, and hopelessly watching the world die year after year. A tragedy carelessly left unsolved.

Jessica Frost (14)
Our Lady & St Bede Catholic Academy, Stockton-On-Tees

THE POISON PERIL

Fog slithered around my feet and covered my surroundings in a thick, eerie blanket. Everything around me was obscured by this misty menace, except for a flicker of orange light amongst the darkness that beckoned me towards it. My curiosity got the better of me. As I took a clumsy, disorientated step forward, a pungent, sickly scent welcomed itself into my nose. Instantly, I recognised the smell. Poison. Not just any poison, but the very poison that wiped out an entire village, including my parents. Terrified. A figure rose from the haze and suddenly, I felt dizzy. I fell. Poisoned.

Ellen Irving (14)
Our Lady & St Bede Catholic Academy, Stockton-On-Tees

THE ABANDONED HOUSE

One evening, I stumbled across an abandoned establishment. I couldn't make out what it was that was in the middle of the forest. As the trees danced in the wind, I heard leaves crunching beneath my feet on a dark November night. The rain began to pour on me. The establishment emerged from the fog and I approached the eerie, abandoned house. Then I knocked on the door. No reply. It was unlocked, so I carefully pushed open the door. I nervously said, "Hello? Is anyone there?" Someone closed the door behind me and replied, "Why, hello there, pretty."

Eva Clydesdale (14)
Our Lady & St Bede Catholic Academy, Stockton-On-Tees

FOLLOWED THROUGH THE ICE

My surroundings were unfamiliar. Nothing I saw was recognisable. The blanket of snow coating everything was no help, but even without, nothing. The beautiful, white, crisp snow seemed to be killing me, its icy coils creeping up my body and squeezing every last bit of soul out of me. Every step felt like it was being watched. I was alone and isolated with only the occasional crow swooping past for company. A noise. Just a snap of twigs, but still a noise. Fear-filled, I could no longer feel the freeze of the deadly snow, just adrenaline. My thought: *run!*

Evie Dixon (14)
Our Lady & St Bede Catholic Academy, Stockton-On-Tees

PLAYING WITH DARKNESS

"Hurry up," the icy wind hissed, pushing him towards the shop's entrance. Nervously, he tried the handle. It immediately swung open with a painful creak. The door slammed behind him, cutting off the flow of the moonlight. It was just him and the darkness, right? His heart screamed otherwise, flooding his insides with frosty blood. "Hello?" Mark's voice echoed. No reply. The silence reassured him - Mark was alone. Well, until he felt their harsh grasp. Claws. Five jagged claws. Suddenly, Mark forgot how to breathe...

Caroline Cummings (14)

Our Lady & St Bede Catholic Academy, Stockton-On-Tees

ALONE

In all honesty, I didn't know where I was. That worried me. It was cold, very cold. Fog was creeping through every alleyway and wind was twisting its way through the trees. There was nobody there. The old, wrecked buildings and towering trees felt as though they were only there to ensure I was scared, as they were barely letting me see the light of day. The silence was deafening. But in the distance, I heard a faint humming sound. It was vibrating through the ground of the abandoned town. All of a sudden, I wasn't on my own anymore...

Abbie Heath (13)
Our Lady & St Bede Catholic Academy, Stockton-On-Tees

THEM

They stood there. My heart pounding, my mind spinning, my stomach twisting. They stood, tall and thin, watching over me. I felt ripples going down my spine. Their eyes. They were black, pulling me as they twisted around and around. My heart raced faster and faster until I opened my eyes. It was all a dream, but the flashbacks were still there. Still trapped, still haunted. I felt something cold... My heart dropped. I couldn't breathe. I felt myself choking and I wasn't dreaming. I was awake and alive with them. It was them...

Nicole Micallef (15)
Our Lady & St Bede Catholic Academy, Stockton-On-Tees

THE DISAPPEARANCE

I woke up to the sound of knocking. *Knock. Knock.* A shiver ran down my spine. I got out of bed. My feet touched the cold, hard, stone floor. I knew something was wrong. I looked over at the bed next to me where my sister slept. Empty! She was gone! My heart was racing as the door creaked open on my way into the hall. I entered the nursery. The rocking chair rocked back and forth on its own. I looked around. The baby was missing. Then I felt a bloody hand over my mouth. Adrenaline filled my body...

Hayley Paskin-Bell (14)
Our Lady & St Bede Catholic Academy, Stockton-On-Tees

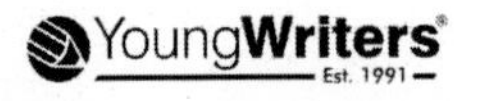

YOUNG WRITERS INFORMATION

We hope you have enjoyed reading this book – and that you will continue to in the coming years.

If you're a young writer who enjoys reading and creative writing, or the parent of an enthusiastic poet or story writer, visit our website **www.youngwriters.co.uk/subscribe** to join the World of Young Writers and receive news, competitions, writing challenges, tips, articles and giveaways! There is lots to keep budding writers motivated to write!

If you would like to order further copies of this book, or any of our other titles, then please give us a call or order via your online account.

Young Writers
Remus House
Coltsfoot Drive
Peterborough
PE2 9BF
(01733) 890066
info@youngwriters.co.uk

Join in the conversation!
Tips, news, giveaways and much more!

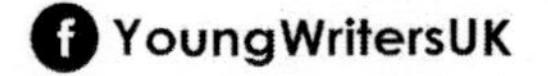

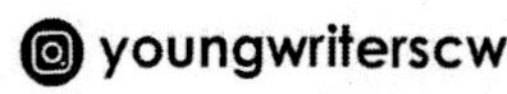